KOALA LOU

WRITTEN BY
Mem Fox

ILLUSTRATED BY
Pamela Lofts

VOYAGER BOOKS • HARCOURT, INC.,

Orlando   Austin   New York   San Diego   Toronto   London

Requests for permission to make copies of any part
of the work should be mailed to the following address:
Permissions Department, Harcourt, Inc.,
6277 Sea Harbor Drive, Orlando, Florida 32887-6777.

Voyager Books is a registered trademark of Harcourt, Inc.

First published in Australia by Ian Drakeford Publishing,
Melbourne 1988
First U.S. edition 1989

The Library of Congress has cataloged the hardcover
edition as follows:
Fox, Mem. 1946–
Koala Lou by Mem Fox: illustrated by
Pamela Lofts.—1st U.S. ed.
p.   cm.
Summary: A young koala, longing to hear her
mother speak lovingly to her as she did
before other children came along, plans to
win her distracted parent's attention.
[1. Mother and child—Fiction. 2. Koala—Fiction.]
I. Lofts, Pamela, ill.   II. Title.
PZ7.F8373Ko   1989
[E]—dc19   88-26810
ISBN 0-15-200502-1
ISBN 0-15-200076-3 pb

TWP   36 35 34 33 32 31
4500258520

Printed and bound by Tien Wah Press, Singapore
This book was printed on Arctic matte paper.

Printed in Singapore

For Lailu and Jan
— M. F.

For Mum and for Gaby
— P. L.

There was once a baby koala so soft and round that all who saw her loved her. Her name was Koala Lou.

The emu loved her. The platypus loved her.
And even tough little Koala Klaws next door
loved her.

But it was her mother who loved her most
of all. A hundred times a day she would laugh
and shake her head and say, "Koala Lou,
I DO love you!"

Whenever she stretched in the early morning sun, or climbed a gum tree, or bravely went down the path all by herself, her mother would smile and say, "Koala Lou, I DO love you!"

The years passed and other koalas were
born — brothers and sisters for Koala Lou.
Soon her mother was so busy she didn't have
time to tell Koala Lou that she loved her.

Although of course she did.

Every night, as she curled up under the stars, Koala Lou thought about the times when her mother had looked at her and said, "Koala Lou, I DO love you!" and she longed for her to say it again. One night Koala Lou had a splendid idea. Preparations had begun for the Bush Olympics. SHE would enter the Olympics! She would compete in the gum tree climbing event, and she would win, and her mother would fling her arms around her neck and say again, "Koala Lou, I DO love you!"

Koala Lou began her training right away.
She jogged and puffed and lifted weights and
panted. She hung from a branch with one claw
at a time till she ached. She did push-ups till
her stomach hurt, and last of all, she climbed
the tallest tree that she could find, over and
over and over again.

Sometimes her mother would watch her and ask, "How're ya goin', blossom?" "Fine, just fine," Koala Lou would reply.

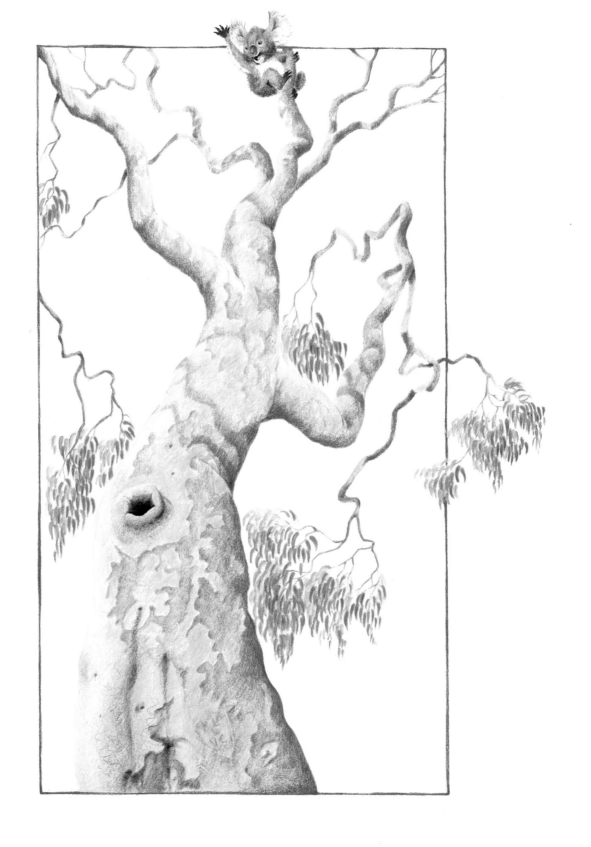

At last the day of the Bush Olympics arrived.

Koala Klaws had also entered the gum tree climbing event and everyone knew how fast she was, but Koala Lou wasn't scared. She saw her mother in the crowd and imagined her saying again, "Koala Lou, I DO love you!" Her heart filled with hope.

It was Koala Klaws who went first. Her climb was a record-breaking twenty-two meters in seventy seconds flat. The spectators whistled and cheered and wildly waved their party hats.

"Can I do better than that?" wondered Koala Lou. "I must." As she stepped toward the tree, a hush fell over the crowd. "On your mark," said the kookaburra. "Get set — GO!"

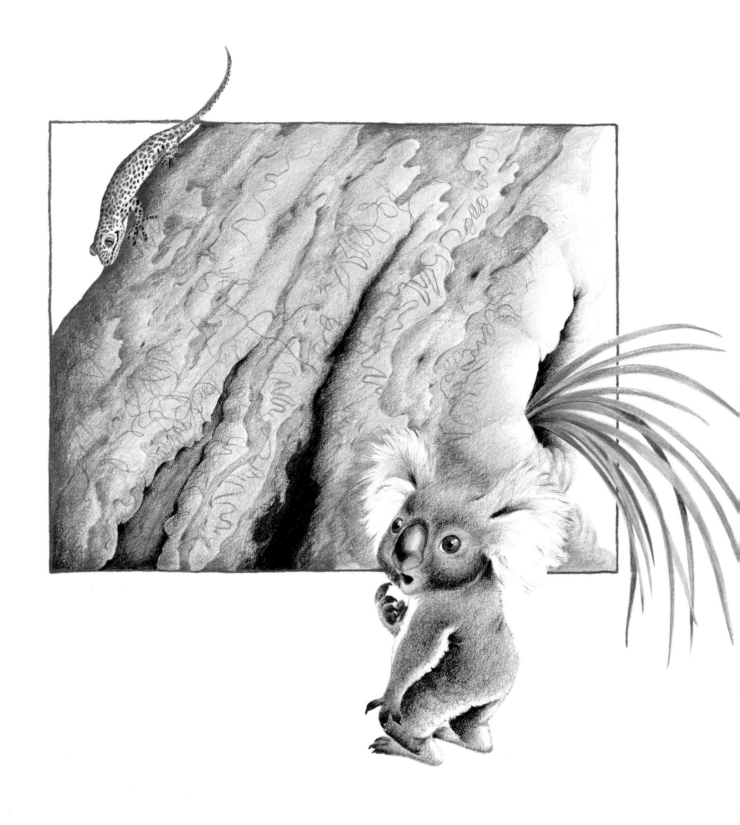

Koala Lou leapt onto the tree. Up and up and up she climbed — higher and higher and higher. Faster and faster and faster until — there she was, right at the very top! The spectators roared and clapped and stamped their feet.

But she wasn't fast enough. In spite of all her training and all her hoping, it was Koala Klaws who won the gum tree climbing. Koala Lou came second.

Koala Lou went off and hid. She heard the
shouts of the Bush Olympics and cried her
heart out.

When the first stars of evening appeared in the sky, Koala Lou crept home through the dark and up into the gum tree. Her mother was waiting for her. Before she could say a word, her mother had flung her arms around her neck and said, "Koala Lou, I DO love you! I always have, and I always will."

And she hugged her for a very long time.